Tootles the taxi and his vehicle friends on land, sea and in the air are all described in rhyming verses and delightfully illustrated to provide lots of amusement for young children.

First Edition

© LADYBIRD BOOKS LTD MCMLXXXIV

All rights reserved. No part of this publication may be reproduced, stored in a retrieval system, or transmitted in any form or by any means, electronic, mechanical, photocopying, recording or otherwise, without the prior consent of the copyright owner.

Tootles the Taxi
and other rhymes

compiled by LYNNE BRADBURY
illustrated by JAMES HODGSON

Ladybird Books Loughborough

*I'm Tootles the taxi,
I'll give you a ride.
Put up your hand,
Then jump inside.
Just watch the meter,
You'll see the fare –
Distance no object –
I go anywhere!*

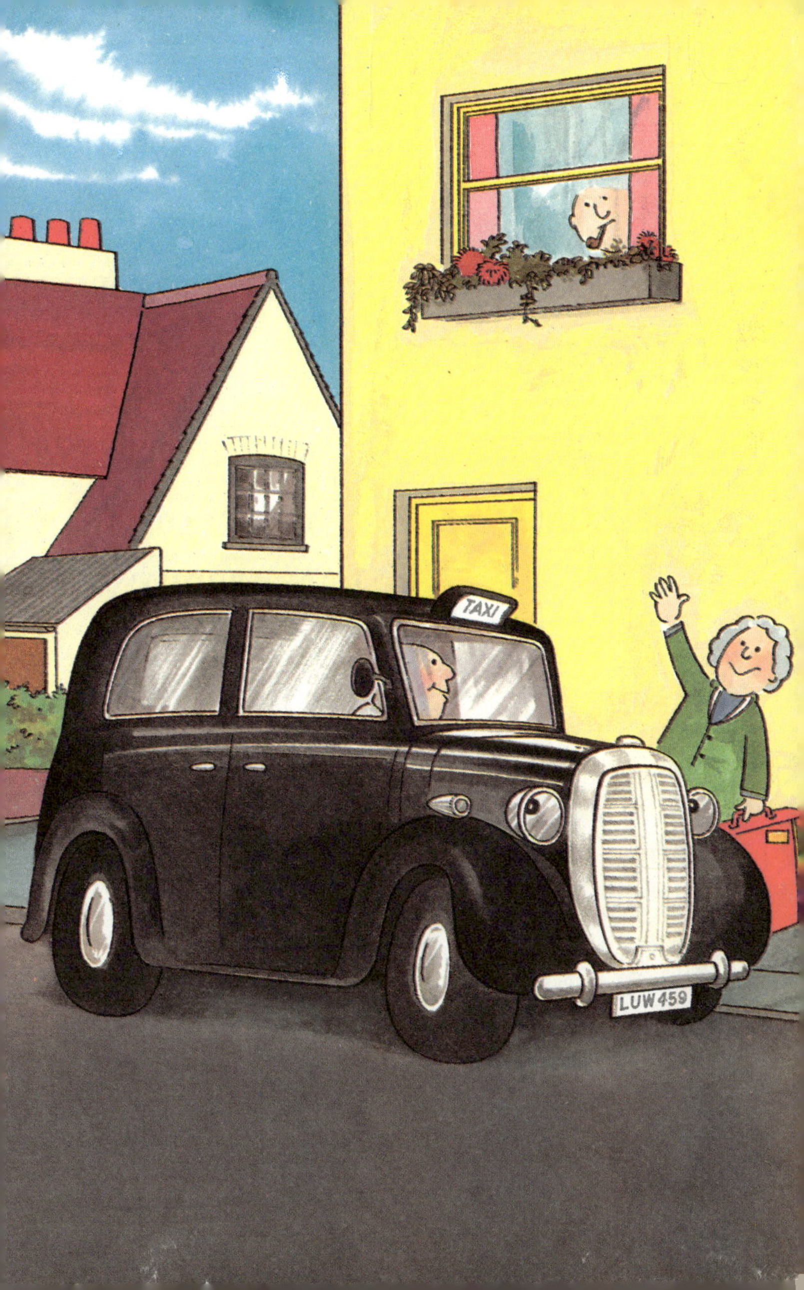
TAXI
LUW 459

*I'm Bertie the bus –
I go from stop to stop,
Carrying the people
To their work or to a shop.
Up and down the streets I go,
Through wind and in the rain,
And back home to my garage
When the night time comes
                      again.*

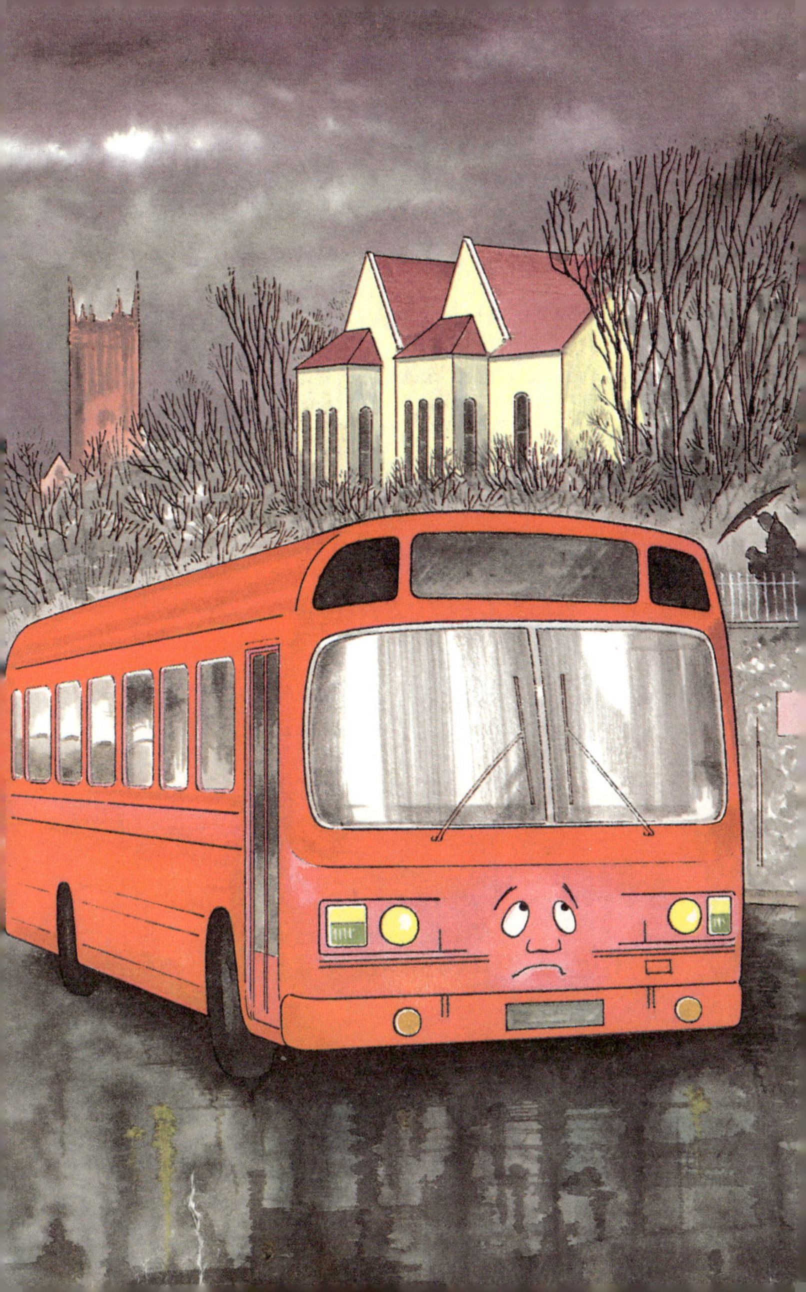

*I'm Archie the ambulance –
By my siren you can tell.
And I've bandages all ready;
A stretcher, as well.
Straight from the hospital,
Or into the town,
To someone who's sick,
Or just been knocked down!*

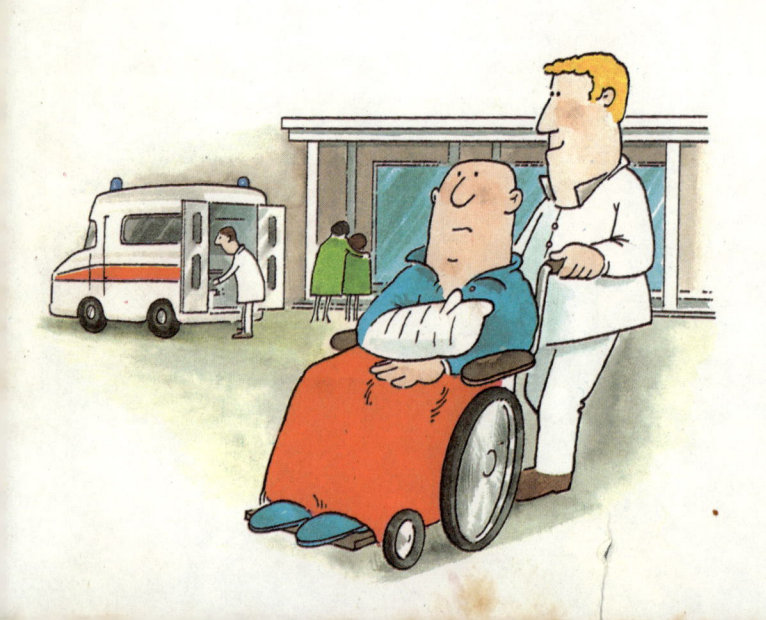

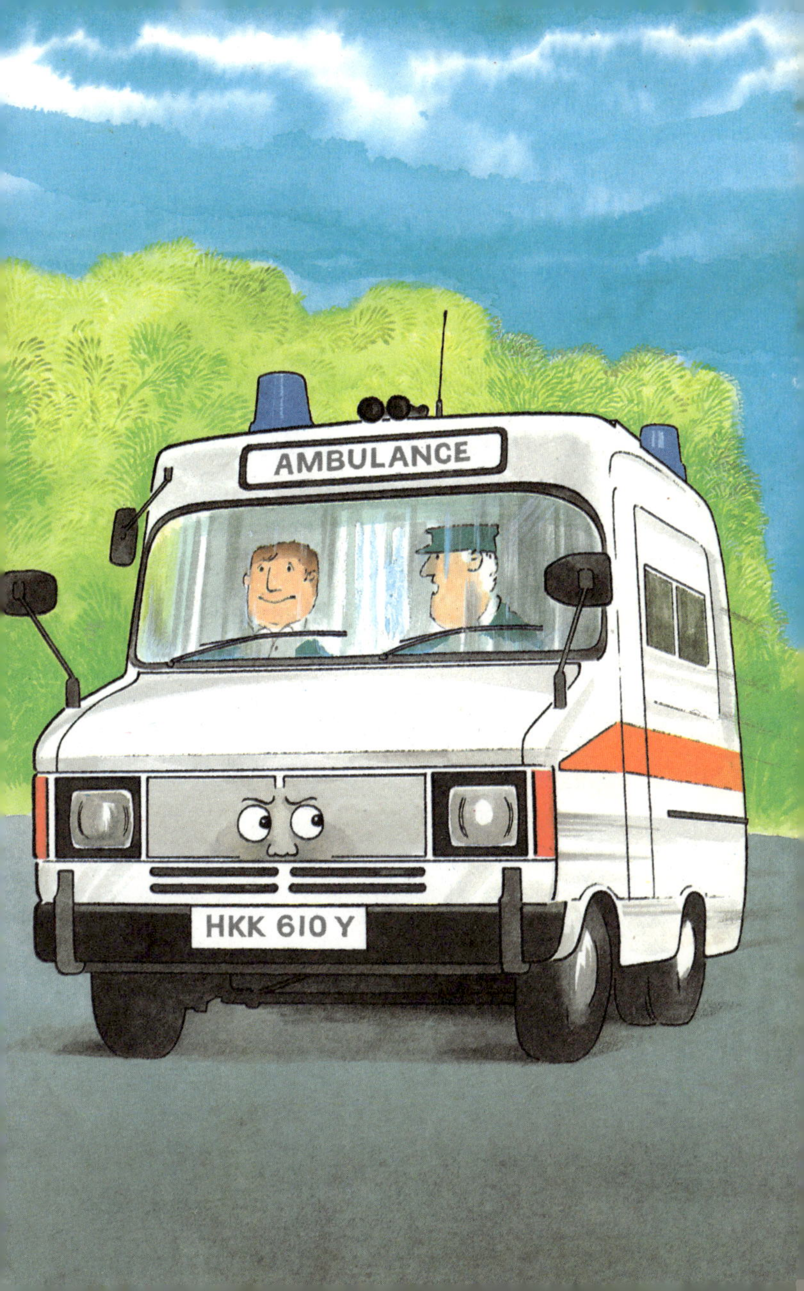
AMBULANCE
HKK 610 Y

I'm Henry the helicopter,
Flying up high;
My big, shiny rotor blades
Going round in the sky.
From here I see traffic jams,
Accidents too –
And over my radio
I tell the police what to do.

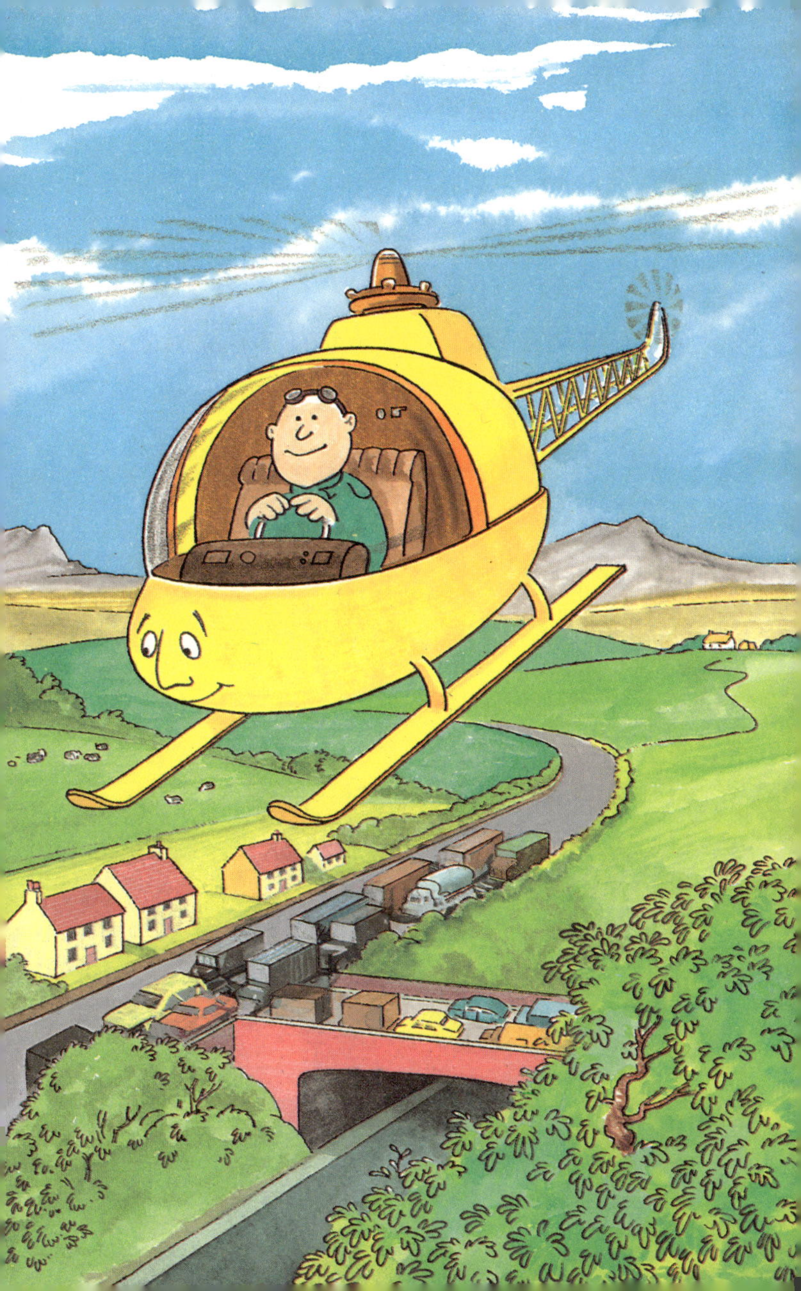

*I'm Tony the tip-up truck,
On building sites I'm found,
Tipping out my load of sand
In big heaps on the ground.
Sometimes it's some timber
I take along the road,
But always I am carrying
A big and heavy load.*

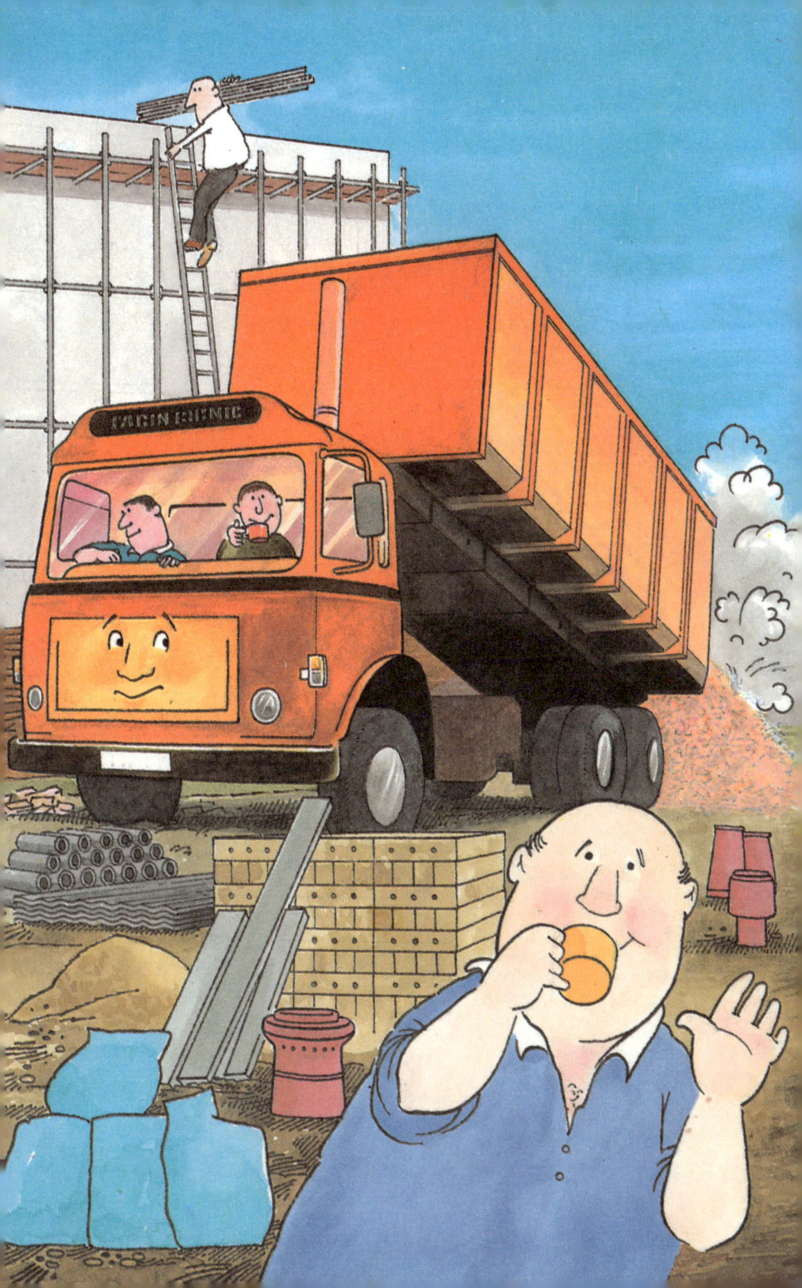

*I'm Mabel the motor coach
Off on my way,
With holiday-makers
All out for the day.
Hear them all laughing
And singing a tune.
Not far to travel—
We'll be there quite soon.*

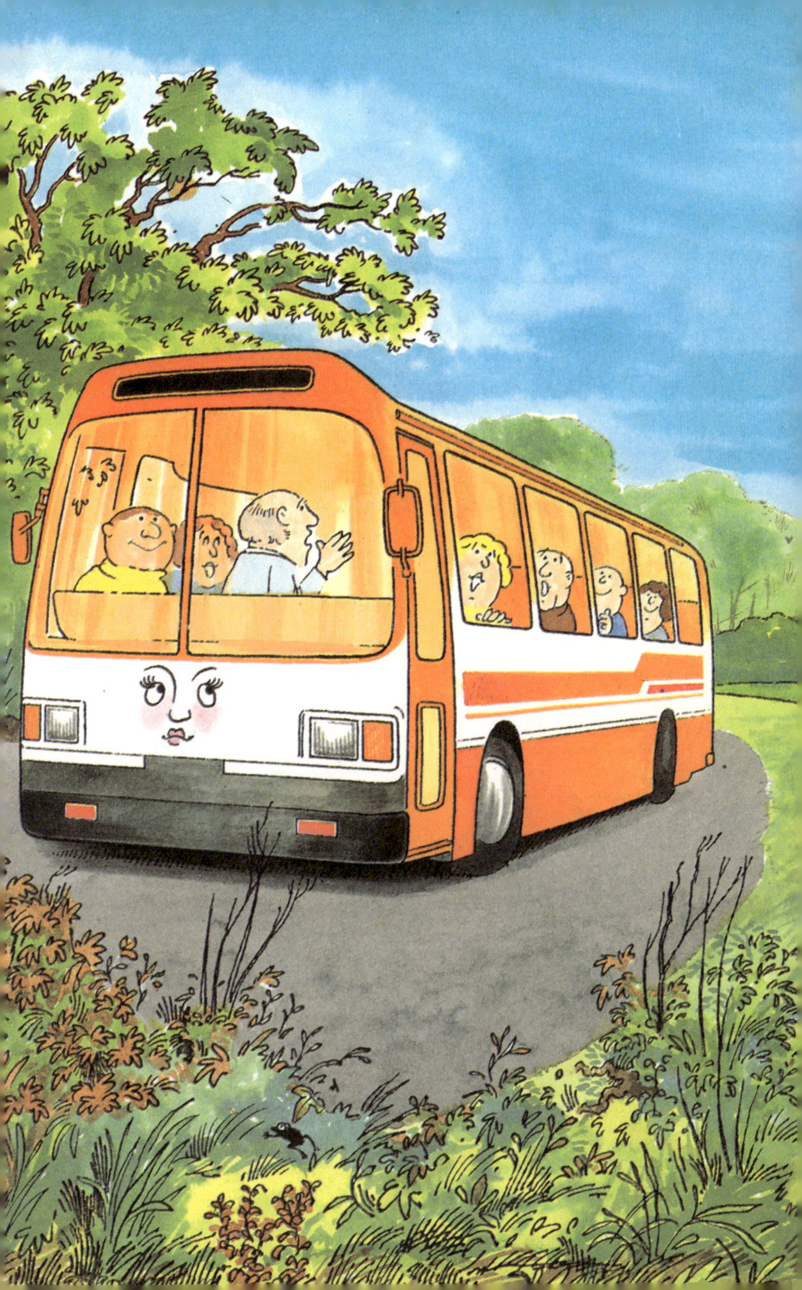

*I'm Billy the bicycle,
Not moving fast;
There's traffic in front
That I cannot pass!
So I'll just be safe
And enjoy the ride,
As I go down the road,
Keeping close to the side.*

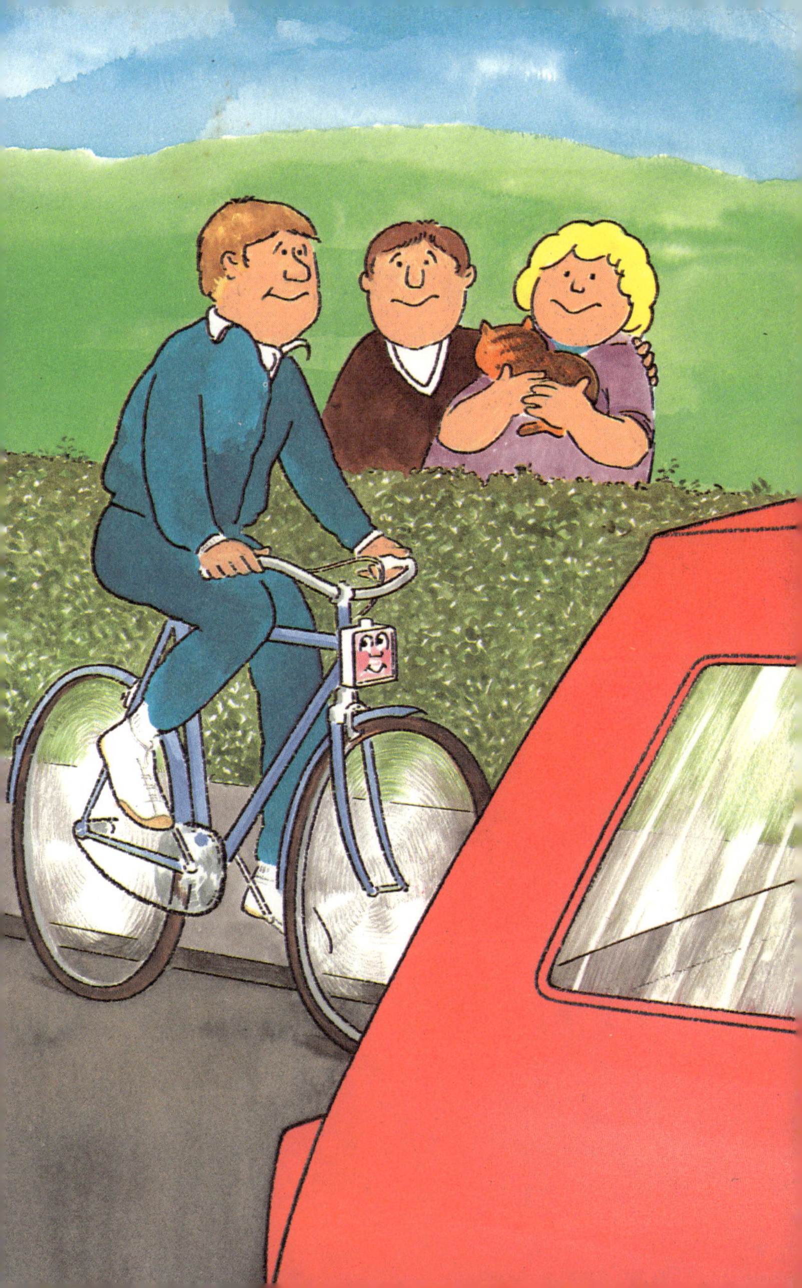

I'm Cathy the car,
A bright shiny blue,
And you'd be surprised
At the things I can do!
I carry five people,
With luggage besides,
And everyone says,
"That was a nice ride!"

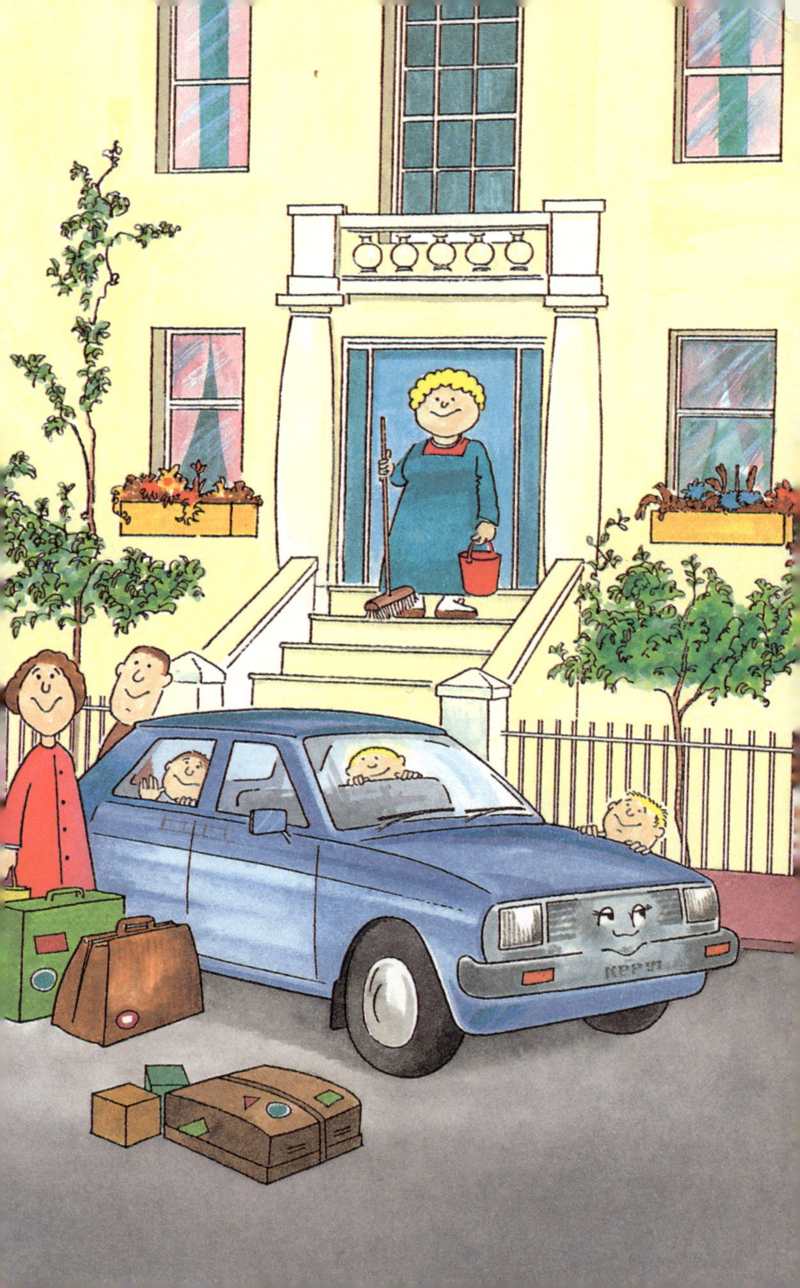

*I'm Boris the bull-dozer;
I know my worth.
When I get to work,
I soon move the earth.
So powerful am I
That no one can say,
I don't earn my rest
At the end of the day!*

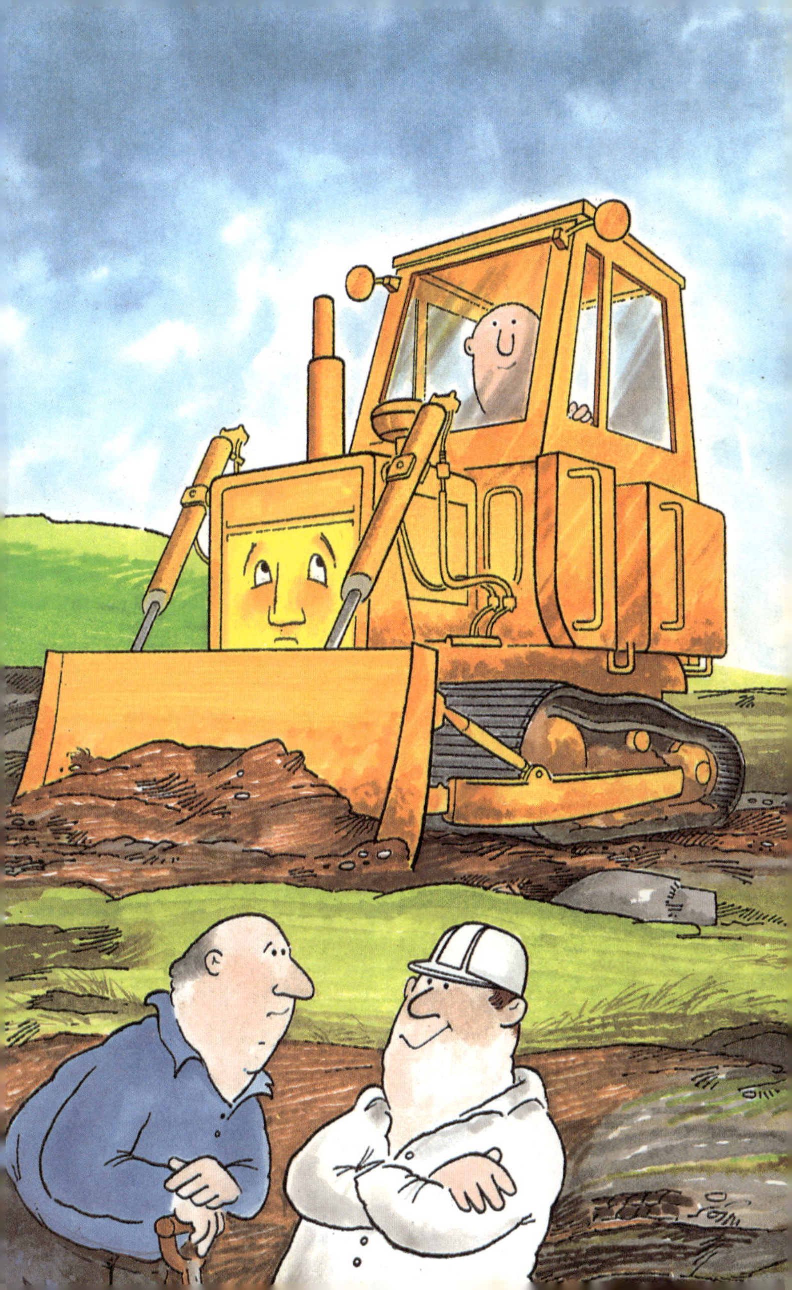

*I'm Mickey the motor-bike
Off to the track.
I go at great speed
And I never look back!
For I am a racer;
I'm one of the best.
I win lots of races
North, South, East and West.*

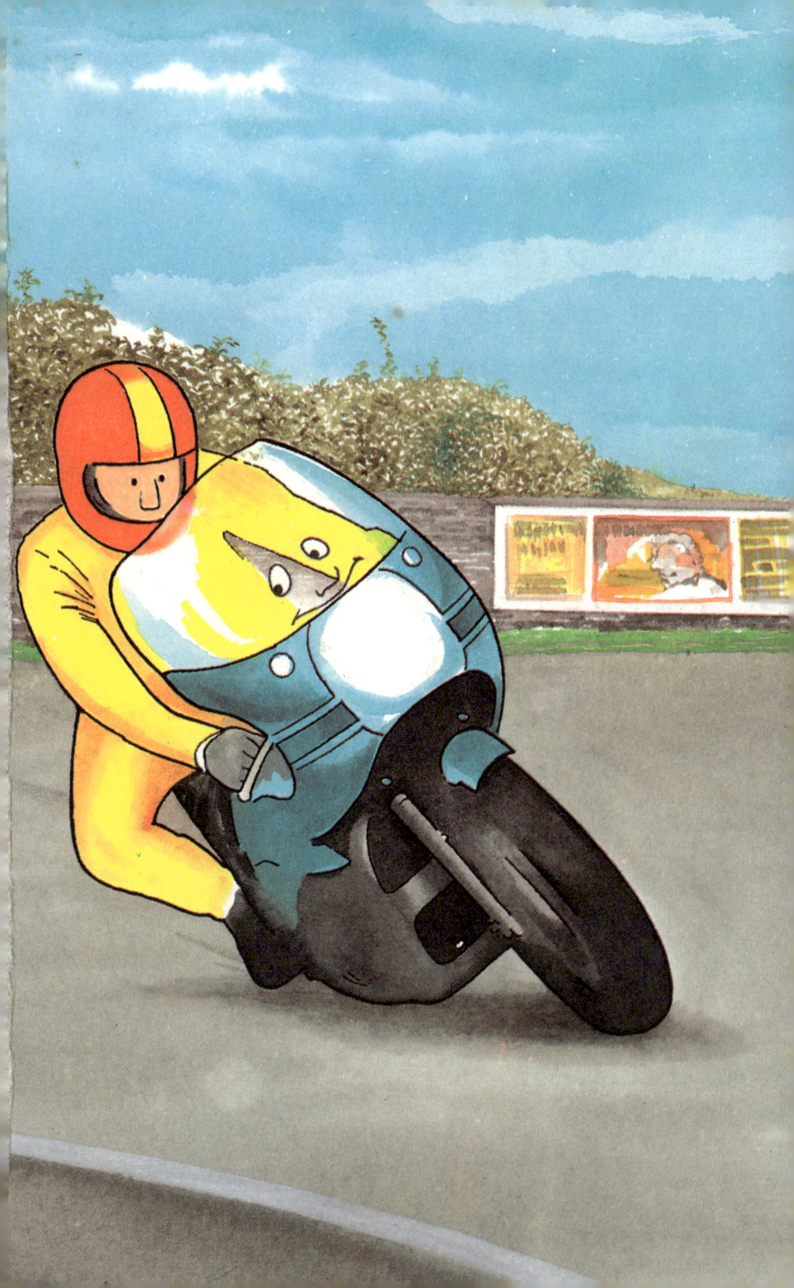

*I'm Trevor the train
And I'm on the right track.
I take people on holiday
And bring them back.
Whatever I carry,
I speed down the line.
Wherever the station,
I get there on time.*

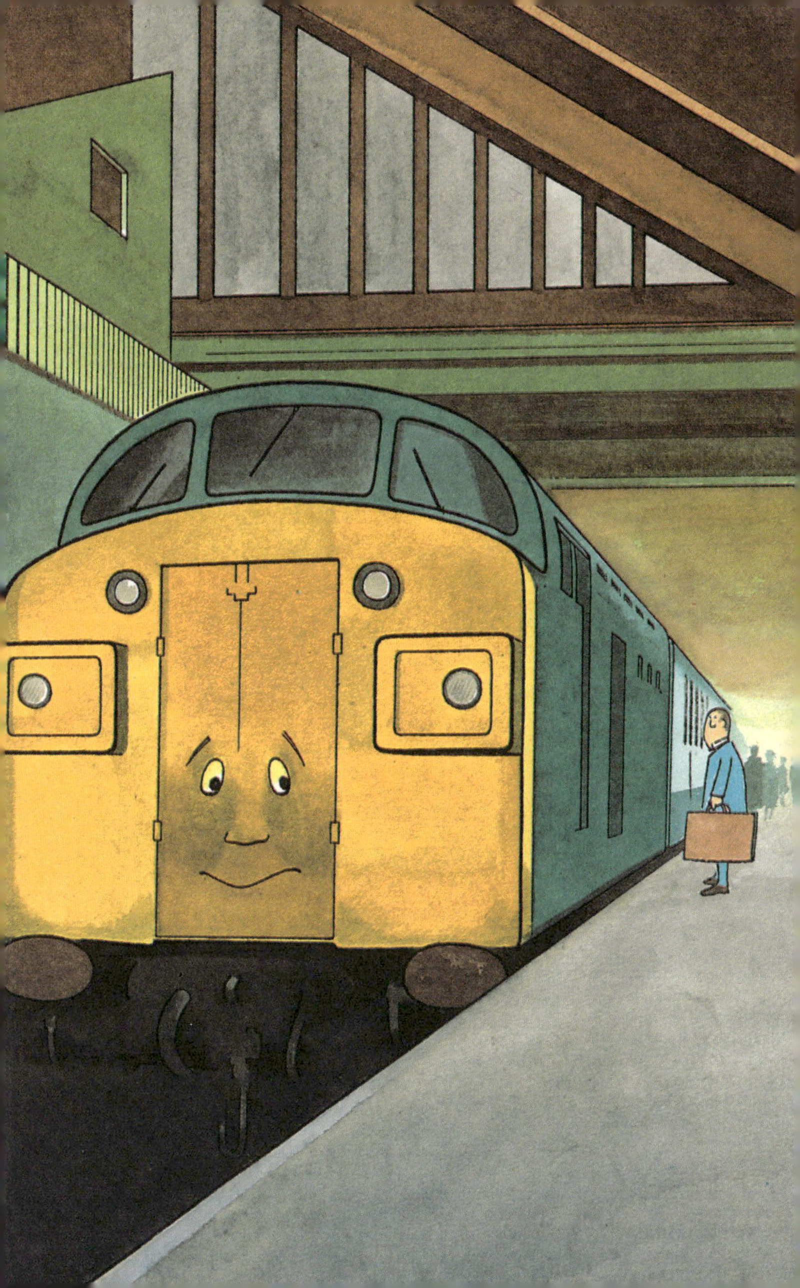

I'm Cuthbert the cattle-truck,
Steady and slow,
Taking the animals
To win at the show.
I'm careful to see that they
Come to no harm,
And drive them back safely
To live on the farm.

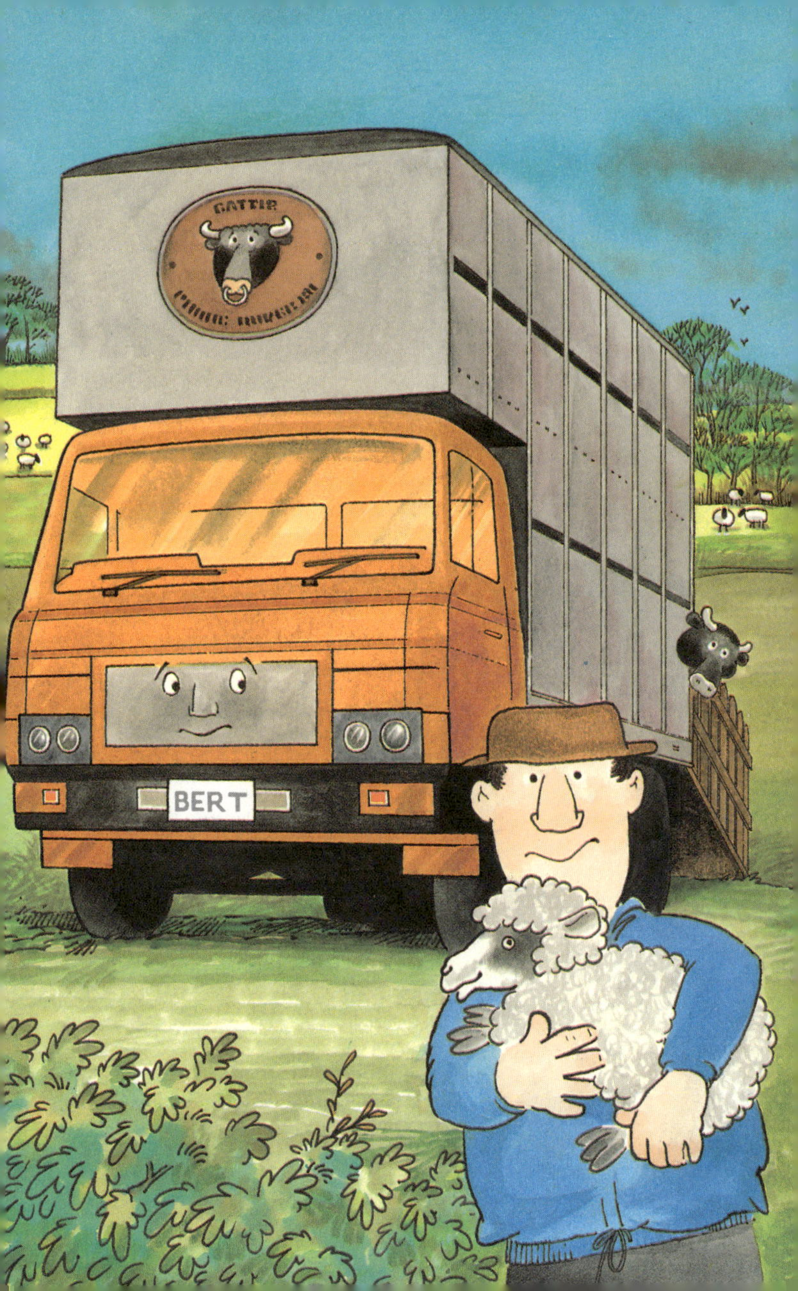
BERT

I'm Freddy the fire-engine
Off to a fire.
I'll soon put those flames out
Before they get higher.
Flashing through town,
Sounding siren or bell,
I carry the firemen
And their hoses as well.

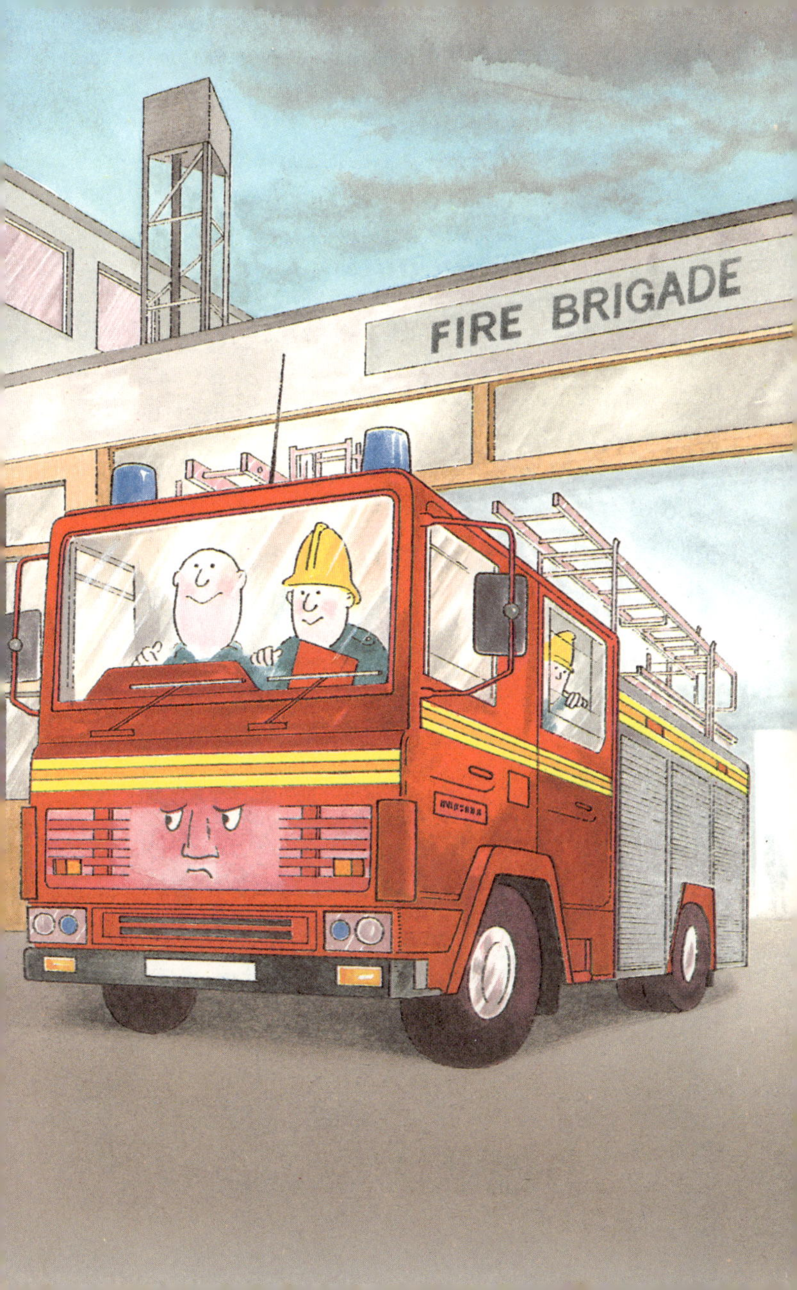
FIRE BRIGADE

*I'm Horace the hovercraft,
Floating on air.
If you want to cross water
Then I'll take you there.
I go very fast
Until I reach land,
Then I come off the water
Straight onto the sand.*

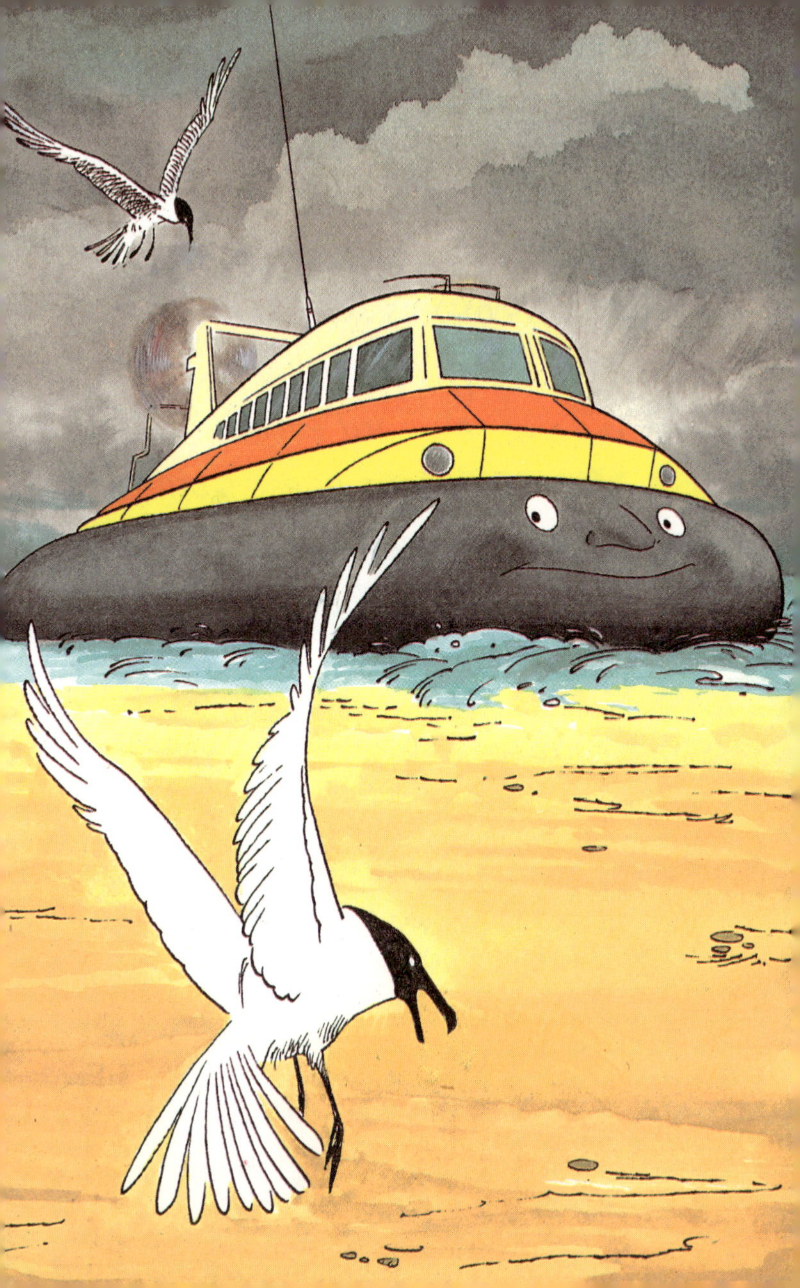

I'm Tommy the tractor.
I work on the land.
The farmer is busy
And I give him a hand.
We dig the hard earth
Making all our lines straight
And often we're working
Until it's quite late.

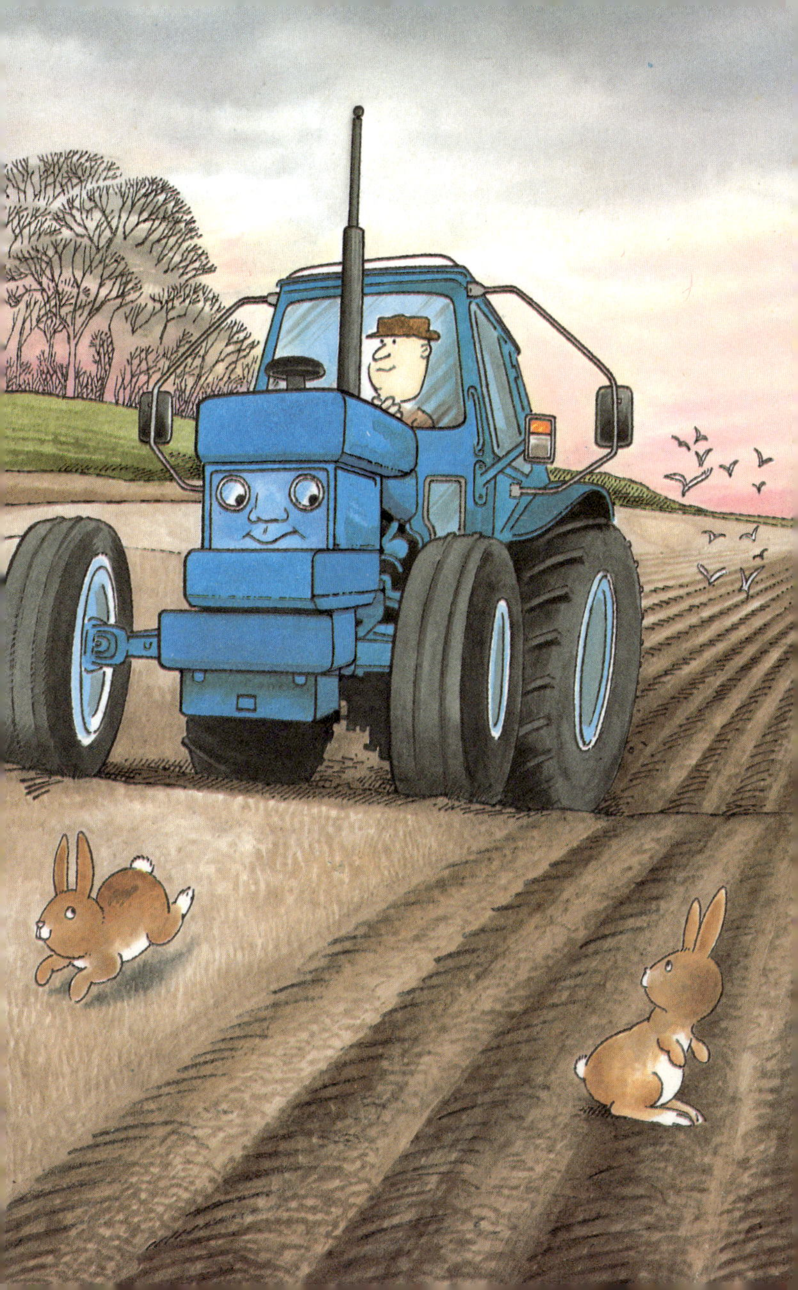

*I'm Terry the tanker,
So heavy and slow;
Filled up to the top
And all ready to go.
When streets are narrow,
I slow down my rate
Because I'm so clumsy
And carry such weight.*

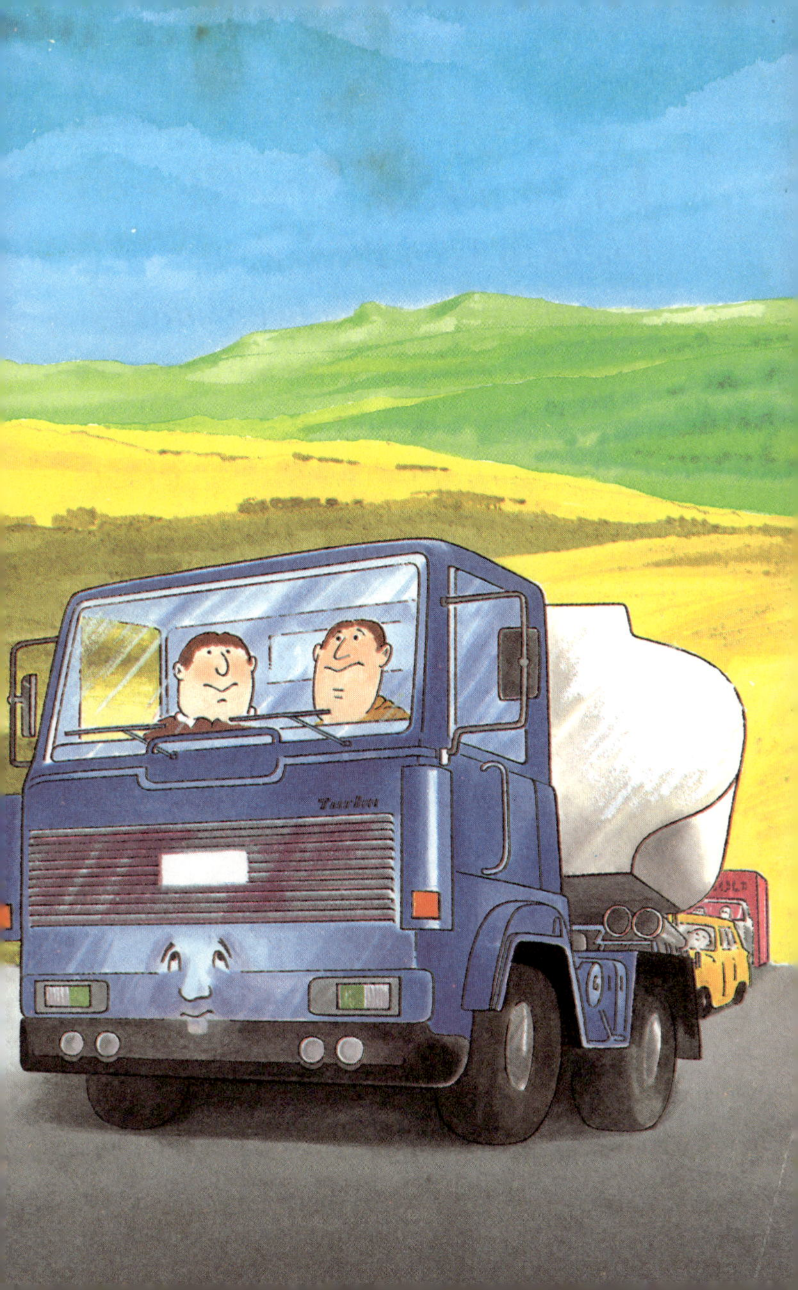

I'm Patrick the police car.
I help to keep the law.
A man rang the police station
About a funny noise next
                door.
Now my lights are flashing;
I'm racing round a bend.
There may have been some
                burglars
And we'll catch them, in
                the end.

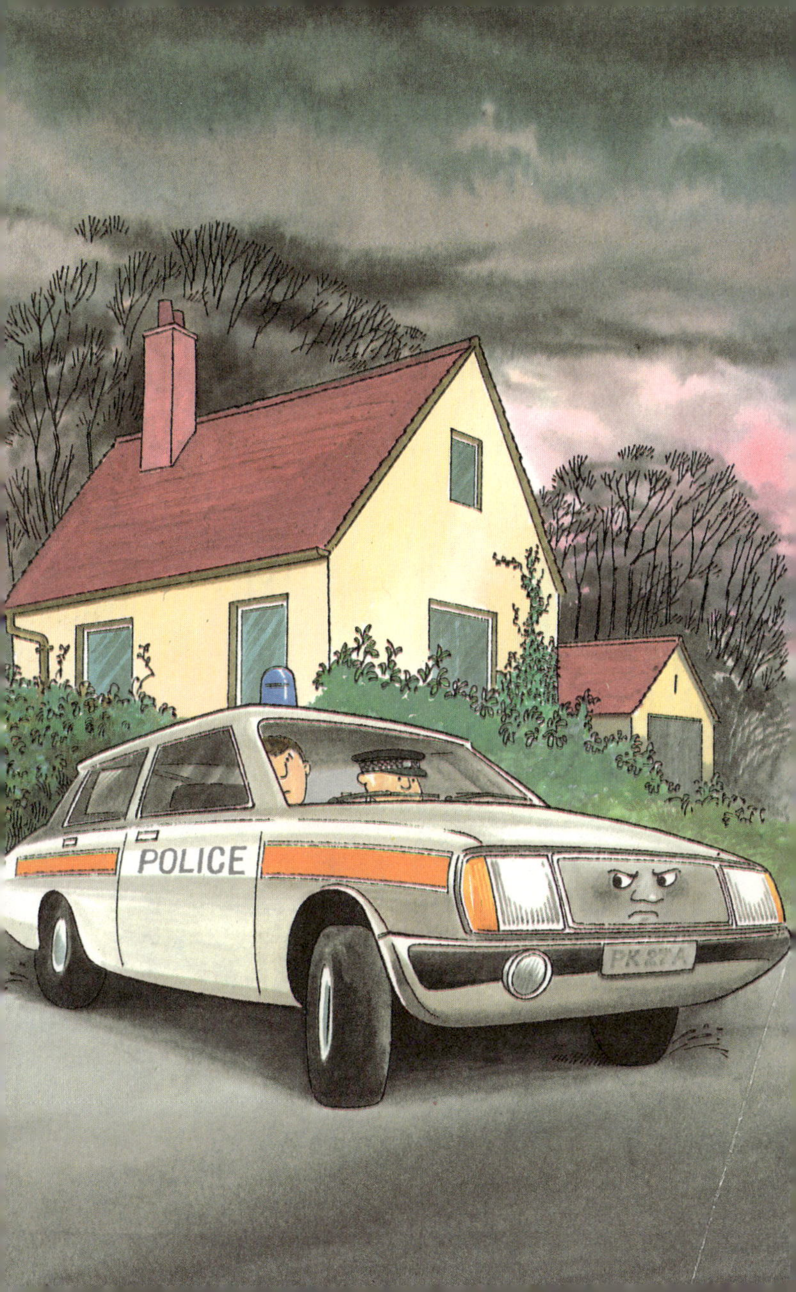
POLICE

I'm Susie the Scooter
And I'm off to the shop.
My basket can carry
All we buy, when we stop.
I'm a pleasure to park
And quite easy to run,
And riding me, everyone says,
Is such fun!

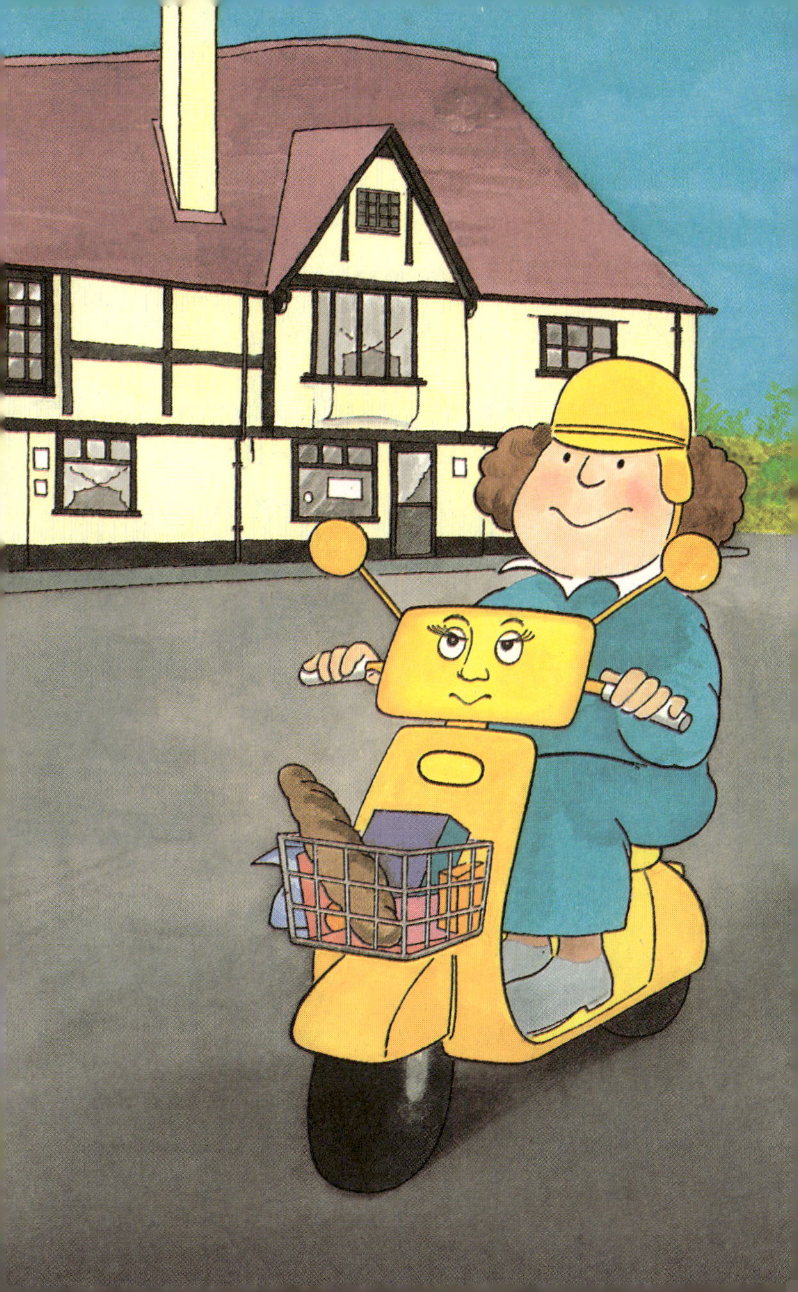

*I'm Tubby the little tugboat
Working in a port.
And though I'm only very
　　　　　　　small,
I pull ships of every sort.
Tugging them and steering
　　　　　　　them,
Safely out to sea,
And though these ships are
　　　　　　very grand,
Each one of them needs me.*

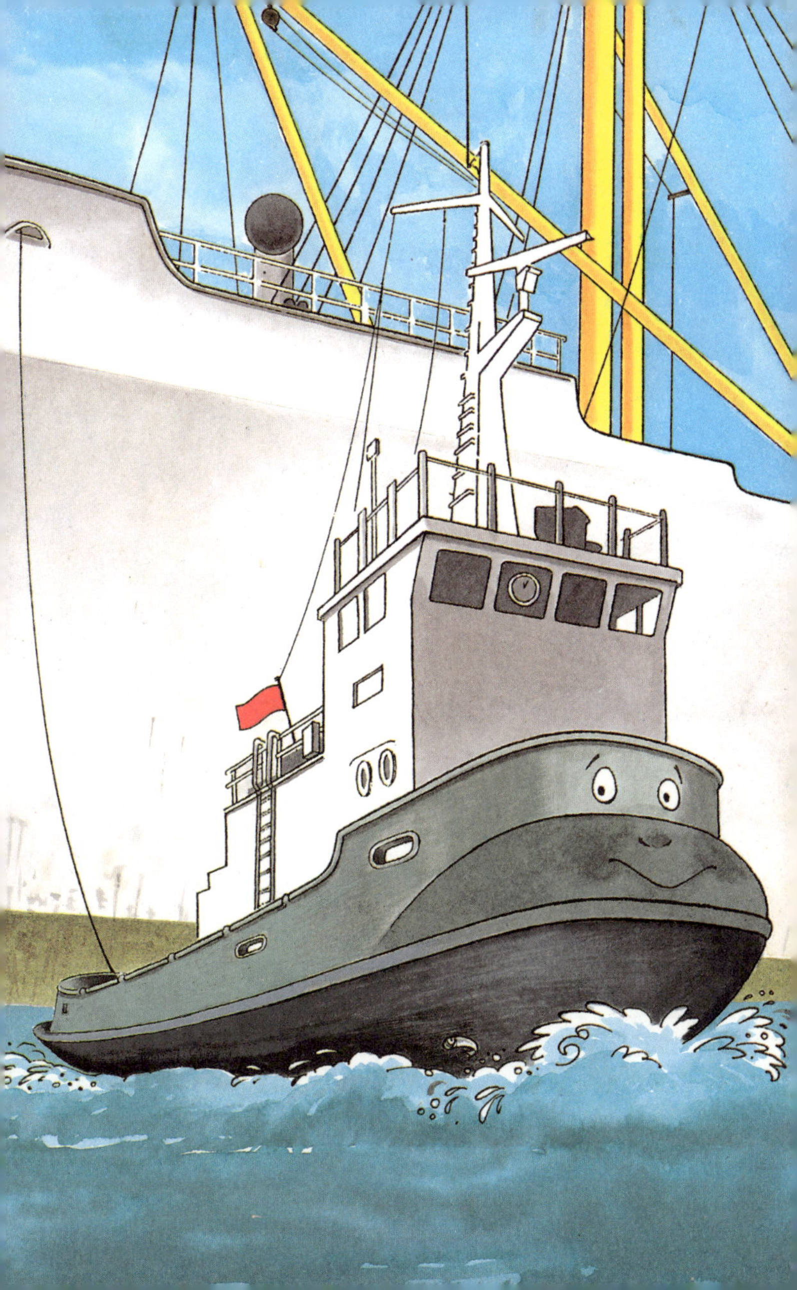

I'm Jerry the jet plane
Getting ready to fly.
I'll be roaring down the
                runway —
Then up into the sky.
I'll fly through fluffy clouds
With all my engines
                humming.
Then I'll radio the airport
To tell them that I'm coming.